Who Says Hoo?

by Kevin J. Brougher & Lisa M. Santa Cruz

WHO SAYS HOO?

Copyright © 2019 Kevin J. Brougher & Lisa Santa Cruz

ISBN# 978-0-9977959-4-3
Library of Congress Control Number : 2019919325

Distributed in United States and Canada by Allied Resources - Abilene Texas.
For wholesale and licensing inquiries, please email
us at : Questions@MissingPiecePress.com

Missing Piece Press, LLC does not accept unsolicited manuscripts.

Visit: MissingPiecePress.com for information on our other fun products.
LIKE us on Facebook to keep up to date with our new books, games and special offers.
"A little Thinking...a LOT of FUN!" is a trademark of Missing Piece Press, LLC.

**Missing Piece Press is a publisher
of award-winning books and games.
Our goal is to produce products that fill the user
with a sense of fun, wonder, and intrigue.**

Other Publications from Missing Piece Press

BOOKS

Thinklers! 1: *A Collection of Brain Ticklers!*

Thinklers! 2: *More Brain Ticklers!*

Thinklers! 3: *Even More Brain Ticklers!*

Thinklers! 4 : *Full-Color Brain Ticklers!*

History Mysteries: *A New Twist on Time-Lines*

State Debate: *50 Unique Playing Cards and 50 Games*

Number Wonders: *A Collection of Amazing Number Facts!*

Dreams, Screams, & JellyBeans!: *Poems for All Ages*

The Storybook: *A novel for ages 10 on up*

Science Stumpers: *Brain-Busting Scenarios...Solved with Science*

Algebra Summary Sheets: *Posters to Promote Proficiency*

Reindolphins: *A Christmas Tale*

Grandpa Kevin's ABC Book: *really kinda strange, somewhat bizarre and overly unrealistic*

GAMES

Frazzle: *A Frenzied Game of Words*

ShanJari: *An African Game of Sequence and Strategy*

Whew! : *Words, Wits, Whims & Woes!*

TooT! : *A Nerdy Little Game*

Blam! : *A Different Card Game*

DICE Blam! : *A Different Dice Game*

Word Nerd : *A Quick-Witted Word Game*

Bunco BUDDIES! : *The BETTER Bunco Game*

Besto : *An Animal Matching Game*

Crummy : *The Criss-Cross Rummy Game*

Take 12! : *The Token Taking Game*

Round About : *A Little Thinking a Lot of FUN!*

.....and more!

A Little Thinking...a LOT of FUN! ™

Missing Piece Press, LLC

Copyright © 2019 Missing Piece Press, LLC   MissingPiecePress.com

For Alexander & Gabriel

Well, for Susie and Pamela, too. Really...it's for any young kid that likes animals.   And...just to be clear, it can be for older kids - I am definitely **NOT** excluding older kids.   You know...it can also be for **ADULTS**.   I mean...hey, I am **NOT** saying adults can't enjoy this. In fact, I think they will. So, I guess, this book is for **EVERY** one out there. But, it's really, uh...mostly for Alexander and Gabriel.   You know...I think it's time to just turn this page and get started.

Enjoy!

Meow, meow - says the cat,
as it stretches in the chair.
Meow, meow - says the cat,
with the fluffy gray hair.

meow
meow

cat

Woof, woof - says the dog,
as it goes to fetch some sticks.
Woof, woof - says the dog.
Now, watch for hugs and licks.

woof
woof

dog

Moo, moo - says the cow,
in the grass so lush and green.
Moo, moo - he's the biggest -
the biggest cow I've seen!

moo
moo

COW

9

Neigh, Neigh - says the horse,
as he munches on some hay.
Neigh, neigh - now it's time -
time to run and play!

neigh
neigh

horse

Chirp, chirp - says the cricket,
in the warm air of the night.
Chirp, chirp - as he stares,
at the moon so big and bright.

chirp
chirp

cricket

Caw, caw - says the crow,
as he flies up over head.
Caw, caw - as he flies
to the nest he calls his bed.

caw
caw

crow

Oink, oink - says the pig - in the mud he rolls around. **Oink, oink** - is the pig's funny grunting sound.

oink
oink

pig

17

Growl, growl - says the bear,
as it rubs against a tree.
Growl, growl - says the bear
as he's running from a bee.

growl
growl

bear

19

Buzz, buzz - says the bee,
as it starts to chase a bear.
Buzz, buzz - says the bee,
as it gets into its hair.

buzz buzz

bee

Screech, screech - says the bat,
as it skims above the lake.
Screech, screech - as it flies
when most are not awake.

screech
screech

bat

Cluck, cluck - goes the chicken,
as it scratches on the ground.
Cluck, cluck - as it eats,
all the things it's found.

cluck
cluck

chicken

25

Click, click - says the dolphin,
as it splashes in the sea.
Click, click - says the dolphin,
so playful and so free.

click
click

dolphin

Quack, quack - says the duck.
as it waddles down the path.
Quack, quack - as it swims
in the lake to take a bath.

quack
quack

duck

Croak, croak - says the frog,
as he sits upon the log.
Croak, croak - then he leaps,
into the muddy bog.

croak croak

frog

Who hoo - says the owl,
with eyes both big and round.
Who hoo - as it flies
with hardly any sound.

who
hoo

owl

Coo, coo - says the pigeon,
as it walks and bobs its head.
Coo, coo - as it finds
some freshly fallen bread.

coo
coo

pigeon

Hiss, hiss - says the snake,
with his tongue he smells the air.
Hiss, hiss - as he slithers,
with no arms - no legs - no hair.

hiss
hiss

snake

37

Hee haw - says the donkey - he works most everyday.

Hee haw - says the donkey - it's also called a "BRAY".

hee
haw

donkey

They all make lots of sounds through out the night and day.

I wonder what it is
that they are trying to say.

But, an elephant so big
   or an ant so very small -
everyone should learn -
   learn to LOVE them ALL!

The end.

For years of family enjoyment get our
award-winning Christmas Tale : Reindolphins

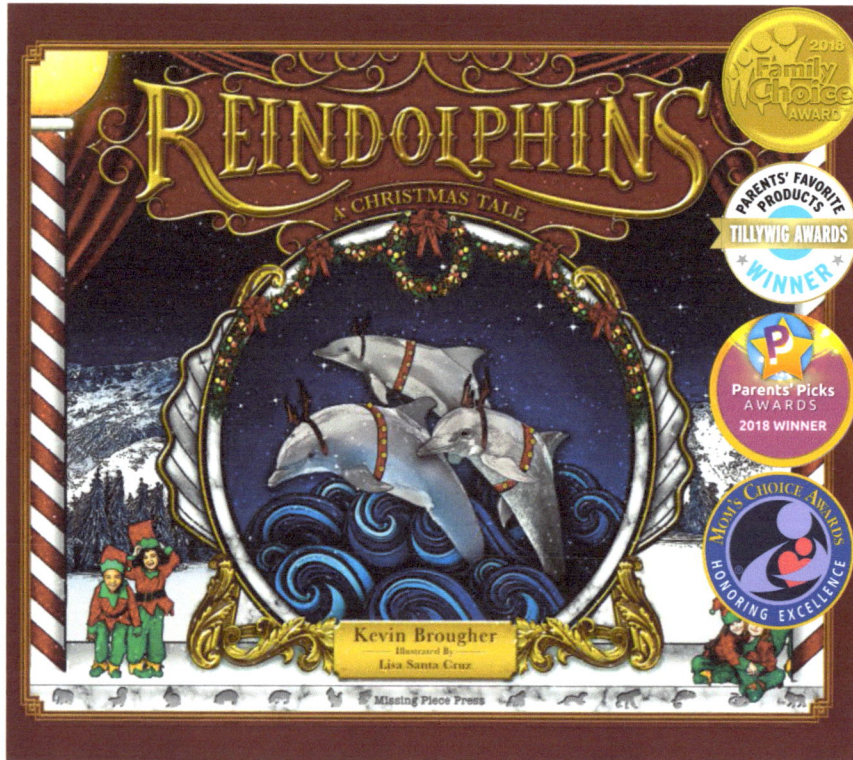

Lots of fun words for young and old.

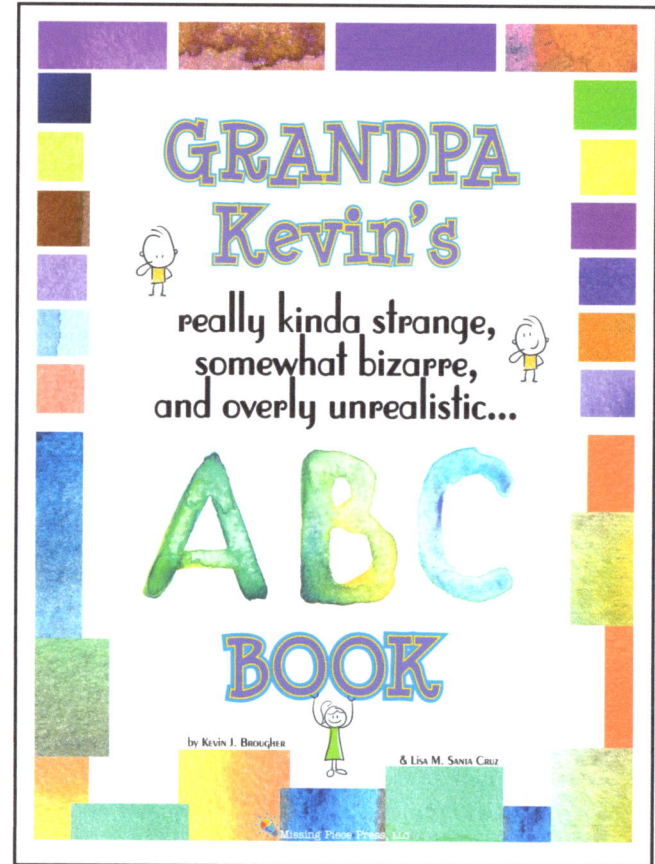

Missing Piece Press, LLC
Copyright © 2019 Missing Piece Press, LLC   MissingPiecePress.com

www.ingramcontent.com/pod-product-compliance
Lightning Source LLC
Chambersburg PA
CBHW040805300326

41914CB00064B/1610